Cocky Colin

Written by Richard Tulloch
Illustrated by Stephen Axelsen

An easy-to-read SOLO
for beginning readers

SOLOS

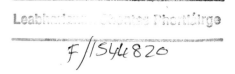

Southwood Books Limited
4 Southwood Lawn Road
London N6 5SF

First published in Australia by Omnibus Books 1999

This edition published in the UK under licence from
Omnibus Books by
Southwood Books Limited, 2000

Cover design by Lyn Mitchell

ISBN 1 903207 18 5

Printed in Hong Kong

A CIP catalogue record for this book is available
from the British Library

Chapter 1

Cocky Colin was the bravest, cheekiest, cockiest cockroach that ever lived.

He could dance and skip and run faster than any cockroach in the world.

Colin's home was a dark place the cockroaches called the Back Off Ridge. There he lived with his mother and father and nineteen brothers and twenty sisters and eighty-one cousins.

But Colin wasn't happy living in the dark.

"I want to dance in the bright light," said Colin. "I want to go where the action is!"

One day, Colin's twenty-seven brothers and thirty-two sisters and one hundred and eight cousins were chewing on a chicken bone that had fallen down the Back Off Ridge.

There wasn't enough for them all
to eat.

Colin said, "I'm hungry. I'm going where the action is!"

He danced out into the bright light.

"Come back, Colin!" called his mother.

"It's dangerous, Colin!" called his father.

But Cocky Colin crawled up the cupboard door to the sunny Kit Chen Bench. He found a strawberry pie topped with whipped cream.

"Yum!" said Colin, and he began to eat.

"Ugh, a dirty cockroach!" yelled a girl. She smacked at Colin with a spoon.

Splat! Cream spurted up into her face. A strawberry stuck on her nose.

Colin skipped left and danced right and ran away to the Back Off Ridge, licking cream from his hairy legs.

Chapter 2

That night, Colin's forty-two brothers and forty-seven sisters and one hundred and thirty-nine cousins were crawling on a dribble of jam in a place they called Be Hind Sink.

There wasn't enough for them all to eat.

Colin said, "I'm hungry again. I'm going where the action is!"

He danced out into the bright light.

"Come back, Colin!" called his mother.

"It's dangerous, Colin!" called his father.

But Cocky Colin climbed up on to the Di Ning Table.

He found a bowl of creamy pumpkin and parsley soup.

"Yum!" said Colin, and he began to eat.

"Ooh, a filthy cockroach!" screamed a lady. She flicked at Colin with a napkin.

Splat! Pumpkin soup splashed into her face. A piece of parsley got stuck in her hair.

Colin skipped left and danced right and ran away to the Back Off Ridge, licking soup from his hairy legs.

Chapter 3

Next morning a man in a green uniform came. He sprayed poison gas and laid sticky traps and left smelly mats by the Back Off Ridge.

That night Colin said to his mother and seven brothers and eight sisters and nineteen cousins, "I'm going away to where the *real* action is – Out Back Door."

"Come back, Colin," called his mother. "It's dangerous!"

But Colin was already out in the street.

Chapter Four

The street was dark, but there was a patch of bright light under a street lamp. In the bright light, in the middle of the road, Colin saw a bag of fatty chips.

"Yum!" said Colin. He danced out on to the road and began to eat.

Brrrrrrmmm! BrrrrrmmmMMMM!

A big truck came round the corner. It was heading straight for Colin.

It ran right across the bag of chips. *Squelch! Splat! Squash!*

Colin skipped left and danced right and ran away towards the gutter, licking fat from his hairy legs.

But then the wind from the truck caught him and tossed him like a leaf, right across the road and *plop!* down a drain.

"Help!" called Colin, but nobody heard.

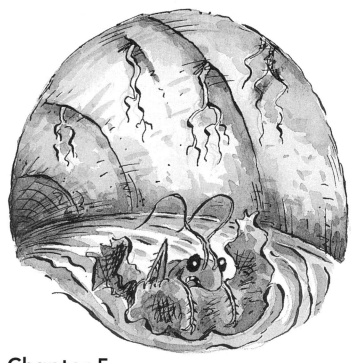

Chapter 5

Cocky Colin clung to a lolly wrapper. Muddy water washed him along the dirty drain.

At last he found a plastic straw and crawled up it. He climbed through a hole into the street again.

Colin saw a bright light coming from a wide doorway. Lots of people were going inside.

"There must be action in there!" said Colin, and he went inside too.

Colin was in a huge hall.

Thousands of people were sitting on seats. They were looking at a brightly lit ring in the middle of the hall.

"That must be where the *real* action is!" said Colin.

Colin crawled right into the middle of the ring, under the bright lights.

All the people cheered.

Cocky Colin thought they were cheering for him, so he did a little dance and took a bow.

But the people weren't cheering for Colin at all.

Chapter 6

They were cheering for the sumo wrestlers!

Two huge sumo wrestlers were climbing into the brightly lit ring. Their legs wobbled. Their arms wobbled. Their tummies wobbled.

The wobbliest wobbly bits of all were their big wobbly bottoms.

Then the sumo wrestlers began to fight.

They pushed and pulled.

They twisted and turned.

They grunted and groaned and stretched and strained.

Their feet stamped to the left of Colin. Colin skipped to the right.

Their feet stamped to the right of Colin. Colin danced to the left.

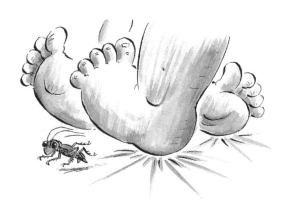

Suddenly one sumo wrestler lifted
the other sumo wrestler up in the air.
The people cheered.

Colin looked up.

Right above him was a wobbly bottom.

Colin skipped and danced, and danced and skipped, and ran around in circles until ...

Chapter 7

Colin opened one eye. His body hurt all over. His right middle leg was missing.

A broom swept him into a dustpan.

The dustpan dropped him into a bin.

The bin was tipped into a truck.

The truck rattled through the streets until it stopped at the Rub Bish Tip.

Chapter 8

Cocky Colin lives on the Rub Bish Tip now.

He has a wife, and two hundred and seven children, and nine hundred and ninety-four grand-children, and eighty-seven thousand, two hundred and fifty-six great-grandchildren.

Every day the sun shines brightly and a line of trucks drops load after load of delicious food in the Rub Bish Tip.

There is plenty for all of them to eat.

When the sun goes down, Cocky Colin does a jerky dance on his five legs.

He tells his family stories about his adventures.

"I've seen the bright lights," brags Colin. "I've been where the action is. I'm the bravest, cheekiest, cockiest cockroach that ever lived!"

He's the luckiest cockroach too.

Richard Tulloch

I've written hundreds of stories for books, plays and TV, but I often get stuck for an idea. One day I was sitting in our kitchen trying to think up a story. Into the middle of the room crawled a big, brave, and maybe very foolish cockroach. Seeing him gave me the idea for this story, so I let him go. Thank you, cockroach!

Later, when I was talking about the idea with some students in a writing workshop, a boy named Finan suggested how the cockroach could get squashed. Thank you too, Finan!

50

Stephen Axelsen

My family and I live in a warm, moist part of the world, so we have lots of cockroaches.

Before I did the drawings for *Cocky Colin* I hated cockroaches. I used to whack them, stamp on them, trap them in sticky traps and poison them with tricky baits. But now I am much nicer to them. I play with them, make them soup and take them for walks.

I was such a meanie before Colin showed me what fine little bugs cockroaches truly are. Thank you, Colin!

More Solos!

Dog Star
Janeen Brian and Ann James

The Best Pet
Penny Matthews and Beth Norling

Fuzz the Famous Fly
Emily Rodda and Tom Jellett

Cat Chocolate
Kate Darling and Mitch Kane

Jade McKade
Jane Carroll and Virginia Barrett

I Want Earrings
Dyan Blacklock and Craig Smith

What a Mess Fang Fang
Sally Rippin

Cocky Colin
Richard Tulloch and Stephen Axelsen